PATCHWORK

HELPS A FRIEND

To my son Finn and husband David,
who show that everything and anything is possible. —J.S.

For Nikolai, Anna, and Colin. —G.G.

Patchwork Helps a Friend

Text © 2013 Gail Greiner
Illustrations © 2013 Jacqueline Schmidt

Published by POW!
a division of powerHouse Packaging & Supply, Inc.

Library of Congress Control Number: 2013934870

37 Main Street, Brooklyn, NY 11201-1021
info@bookPOW.com
www.bookPOW.com
www.powerHouseBooks.com
www.powerHousePackaging.com

ISBN: 978-1-57687-642-8

Book and Jacket design by Jacqueline Schmidt and J. Longo

10 9 8 7 6 5 4 3 2 1

Printed in China

PATCHWORK
HELPS A FRIEND

WRITTEN BY GAIL GREINER   ILLUSTRATED BY JACQUELINE SCHMIDT

Patchwork is a hodgepodge, part patches, part bear;
Patchwork's friend Fred is in need of repair.

"Can you help me help Fred?" Patchwork asked Raccoon.
"Take this rag, it's all yours—but I'm busy this afternoon."

"Can you help me help Fred?" Patchwork asked Blue Whale.

"Why of course, use this thread. Now I must get my mail."

"Can you help me help Fred?" Patchwork asked Narwhal.

"Look in my chest, help yourself! I'm expecting a call."

"Can you help me help Fred?" Patchwork asked Starling.
"These towels will do. Run along, you're a darling."

"Can you help me help Fred?" Patchwork asked Mule.
"What's mine is yours! Goodbye, I'm late for school."

A friend in need

is a friend indeed.

"Can you help me help Fred?" Patchwork asked Fawn.
"Use this bag. It's my nap time," she said with a yawn.

"Can you help me help Fred?" Patchwork asked Llama.
"This scarf is for you. Oh! I think I hear Mama!"

"Can you help me help Fred?" Patchwork asked Bear.
"You can have this old sweater, but I'm late for the fair."

"Everyone's so busy," said Patchwork, scratching his head.
"But they gave me everything I need to help my friend Fred."

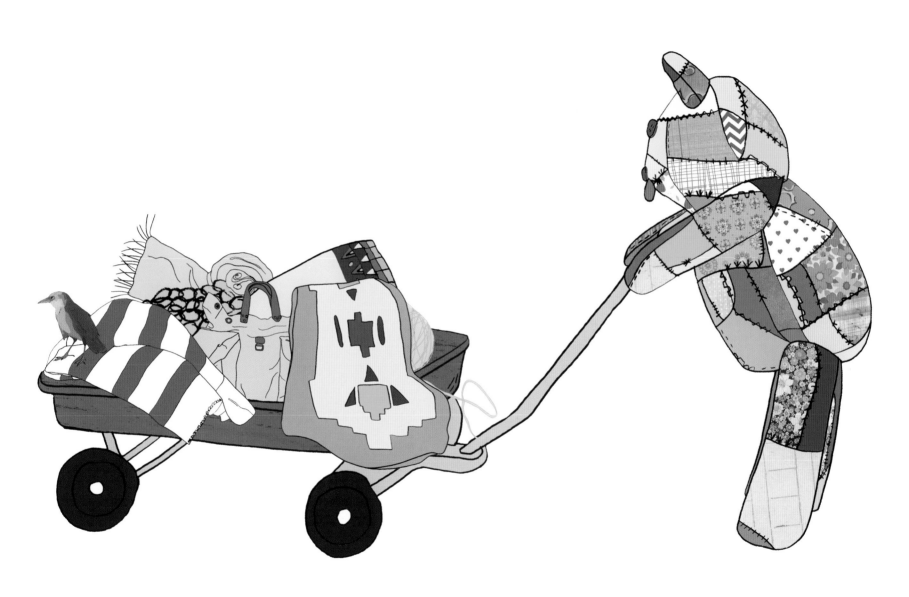

So Patchwork took the sweater, the scarf, and the bag,
the towels, the treasure, the wool, and the rag.

He brought it all to his workshop to fix his friend Fred,
but he felt so tired from his day, he fell fast asleep on his bed.

Patchwork dreamed of a trek to Peru.
When he awoke, he saw Fred all patched up, as good as new.

"Surprise!" shouted Bear, Llama, Fawn, Mule, Starling, Narwhal,
Blue Whale, and Raccoon, "We've been working on Fred all afternoon!"

Patchwork is a hodgepodge, part patches, part bear;
Patchwork and Fred, an old patchwork pair.

Let's dance!